Same Idea, Different Year

Written by Susan Griffiths

Illustrated by Trish Hill

Contents	Page

Same Idea, Different Year

With these characters ...

Jim

Jemma

Melba

Rosie

"You're going to be late

Setting the scene ...

Messy bedrooms, dogs hiding shoes, running late for school — and homework! In these two stories from different years, we see that while many things have changed, some things never do!

And two children from different years even share the same idea about what they want to do when they are older.

for school again!"

Chapter 1.

"Golly! What a stink!"

Jim lay on the floor. Something smelled very peculiar under his iron bed. He saw a pile of wooden toys, books, and cowboy comics. Jim used his wooden ruler to pull out a pair of unwashed woolen socks. He hadn't worn them for months! Yuck!

Chapter 1.

"Yuck! How gross!"

Jemma lay on the floor. Something smelled disgusting under her bed. A pile of CDs, books, and pop music magazines lay there. Jemma moved the things with her plastic fairy wand. She found a pair of unwashed and very smelly nylon socks. Yuck!

"No time to find a clean pair! Now, where is my other boot?" Jim thought. He was already running late for school without having to do a boot search! Where was it?

As usual, Jim's room was a mess. He knew this would upset his mother, so he pushed everything under his bed.

In a rush, Jemma put on the smelly socks. "Where's my other running shoe?" she hissed. She was already running late for school. Where was it?

"No time to clean up this mess before school," she sighed. Instead, she shoved everything under her bed. "A missing shoe and smelly socks are so uncool!" she told herself.

Jim limped over to the washstand. There, he washed his hands with homemade soap and cold water from a jug. Melba, the dog he had named after a popular singer, looked up at him.

After quickly combing his hair, Jim followed the delicious smell of bacon and freshly laid eggs frying in the kitchen.

Jemma limped as fast as she could to the bathroom. There, she turned on the hot and cold faucets to fill the sink with warm water and soap. Rosie, the dog she had named after a popular singer, peeked around the door.

After quickly rubbing hair gel through her hair, she followed the music blaring from the radio in the kitchen.

"Good morning, Jim," said his mother, warmly. She was washing dishes in the sink. The wood stove heated a black iron kettle and warmed the kitchen air. Jim spread his toast with freshly-made butter, and then ate his bacon and eggs.

As Jim's mother looked up at the clock, she sniffed deeply and said…

"Good morning, Jemma," said her dad, cheerily. While the coffee was dripping, he loaded the dishwasher. The gas furnace warmed the kitchen air. Jemma started eating her breakfast of granola, yogurt, and fruit.

As Jemma's father looked over at the digital clock on the microwave, he sniffed deeply and said…

Chapter 2.

"What's that peculiar smell?
And where's your other boot?" asked
Jim's mother. "You're going to be late
for school again!"

Jim stood up and noticed his missing
boot lying on the ground by the hens.
What a relief! He knew that Melba had
been playing with his boot again!

Chapter 2.

"What's that disgusting smell?
And where's your other shoe?" asked
Jemma's dad. "You'll be late again!"

Jemma stood up and noticed her
other running shoe lying next to her
sleepy black cat. Cool! She told
Rosie she was a bad dog for
taking her shoe outside.

Jim raced outside and quickly put on his boot. "Good-bye, Mother!" he called, as he dashed through the long grass. Melba ran on ahead.

Two mules pulling a cart appeared over the hill. Jim's father waved.

"Are you late for school again? I've been up for hours!" his father called.

Jemma raced outside to grab her running shoe. She hurried upstairs to grab her school bag. But something on the TV in her room caught her attention. Jemma sat, fascinated by what she saw.

As she watched TV, Jemma heard the hum of her mom's car. She was a doctor and had been working at the hospital since midnight.

Jim climbed over fences and sprinted through paddocks. When he was almost at the school gate, he heard a strange roar behind him.

Skidding to a stop, he turned around. The sound roared closer and closer. Jim squinted as he looked up at the sky. He saw the most amazing sight he had ever seen!

"You're late again!" called Jemma's mom, as she headed for the shower. "Turn that TV off and go to school!"

Jemma waved, but she could not take her eyes off the TV.

On the TV, she saw the most amazing sight that she had ever seen.

Chapter 3.

A red airplane was flying high above Jim.
It was the most amazing sight!
Its wings shined brightly in the sunlight.
Its engine made a sound like thunder.

The airplane zoomed overhead, and
Jim watched as it slowly became smaller
and smaller.

Chapter 3.

On Jemma's TV, a gleaming space
shuttle was ready for take-off. Numbers
on the TV counted down to zero. Then
Jemma saw a burst of flames and heard
the rocket engines roar.

From within the clouds of smoke,
the space shuttle sped upward and
into the sky.

The sun flashed on the airplane's wings as it turned and circled back toward Jim. The noise grew louder again, and the airplane zoomed over Jim once more.

Jim had read about airplanes in his books, but had never seen or heard a real one. This flying machine was incredible!

Jemma's eyes hardly blinked as she watched the shuttle race toward space.

For weeks, the TV, radio, and newspapers had been reporting on the first space mission to send people to Mars. And now it was happening! The astronauts were leaving on the first stage of their two-year long journey.

"Wow! Imagine flying faster than a bird!" Jim said, jumping up and down excitedly. He imagined being a pilot with the wind skimming past his face, surrounded by loud engine noises.

The school bell ringing in the distance brought Jim back to the real world. Oh, dear! Jim knew he would be in trouble again!

Jemma imagined being an astronaut inside the speeding shuttle, surrounded by loud engine noises. Jemma wondered what it felt like to be weightless and to see the earth as a small, blue circle.

Suddenly, the beeping of her digital watch brought her back to earth.
Nine o'clock already? Jemma was going to be in trouble again!

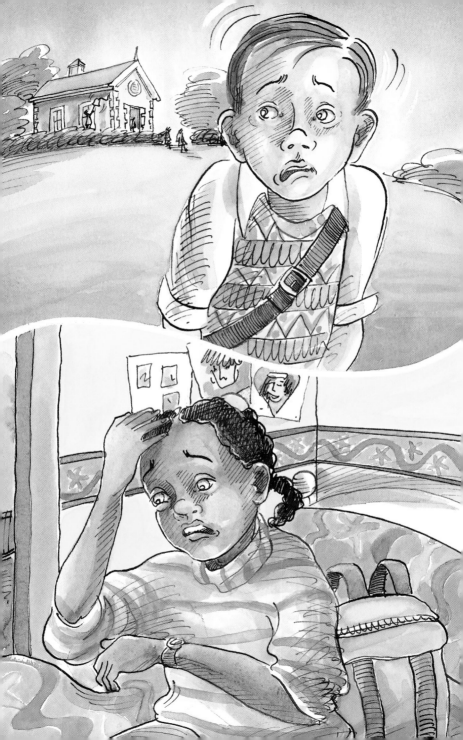

Chapter 4.

That afternoon, Jim's teacher kept him late. Jim sat alone, writing one hundred lines, each one saying, "I must not be late."

Now Jim would be even later getting home to do his chores: feeding the hens, bringing in coal for the fireplace, and brushing down the horses.

Chapter 4.

After school, Jemma had to do extra math in class. Instead, she drew pictures of space shuttles.

She wondered how she would explain being late to do her chores: feeding her pets unloading the dishwasher, doing her laundry and checking the computer for e-mails.

That evening, as Jim's family listened to their radio, his imagination took him hundreds of miles up in the air. In his mind he became a pilot, zooming high above the fields and waving at the tiny people below!

Suddenly, his thoughts were interrupted.

That evening, Jemma's family watched the TV in the living room. But Jemma's imagination took her thousands of miles above the earth. How fantastic it would be to become an astronaut and explore planets millions of miles from Earth!

Suddenly, her thoughts were interrupted.

"Jim, didn't you hear what I said? Please do your homework," said his father.

"But, Father, I had to write a hundred lines *and* do all my chores," said Jim, grumbling. His father shook his head.

Jim groaned and trudged over to the table. He always had too much homework.

"Jemma, are you listening? I said it's time for homework," said her mother.

"But, Mom, I've already done heaps of math *and* all my chores," Jemma grumbled. Her mother shook her head.

Jemma trudged over to the desk and switched on the computer. She always had too much homework.

"It's not fair," thought Jim. "Won't adults ever learn that there are better things to do than homework?"

Jim smiled to himself. "Things like dreaming about the day *I* become a pilot!"

"It isn't fair," Jemma thought. "Won't adults ever learn that there are better things to do than homework?"

Jemma smiled to herself. "Things like dreaming about the day *I* become an astronaut!"

"Late!"

I've lost my boot, my socks do smell,
There's a mess under my bed!
I'm late again, but what's that noise?
An airplane, bright and red!

Because I was late, I spent my day
Dreaming of space and stars!
When I'm older, no homework *then*,
For this astronaut to Mars!